# ART

• PATRICK McDONNELL •

 LITTLE, BROWN AND COMPANY
New York ~ Boston ~ London

Also by Patrick McDonnell: *The Gift of Nothing*

Text and Illustration copyright © 2006 by Patrick McDonnell     All rights reserved.

Little, Brown and Company   •   Time Warner Book Group   •   1271 Avenue of the Americas, New York, NY 10020   •   Visit our Web site at www.lb-kids.com

Library of Congress Cataloging-in-Publication Data: McDonnell, Patrick. Art / Patrick McDonnell.— 1st ed.     p. cm.

Summary: A rhyming tribute to a budding young artist.   •   ISBN 0-316-11491-X

[1. Drawing—Fiction. 2. Play on Words—Fiction. 3. Mother and child—Fiction. 4. Stories—Fiction.] I.Title.

PZ8.3.M459548Art 2006     [E]—dc22     2005007975

First Edition: April 2006     10 9 8 7 6 5 4 3 2 1     PHX     Printed in the U.S.A     Printed on recycled paper

# THIS IS ART

# AND THIS IS ART

# ART AND HIS ART

CAN YOU TELL THEM APART?

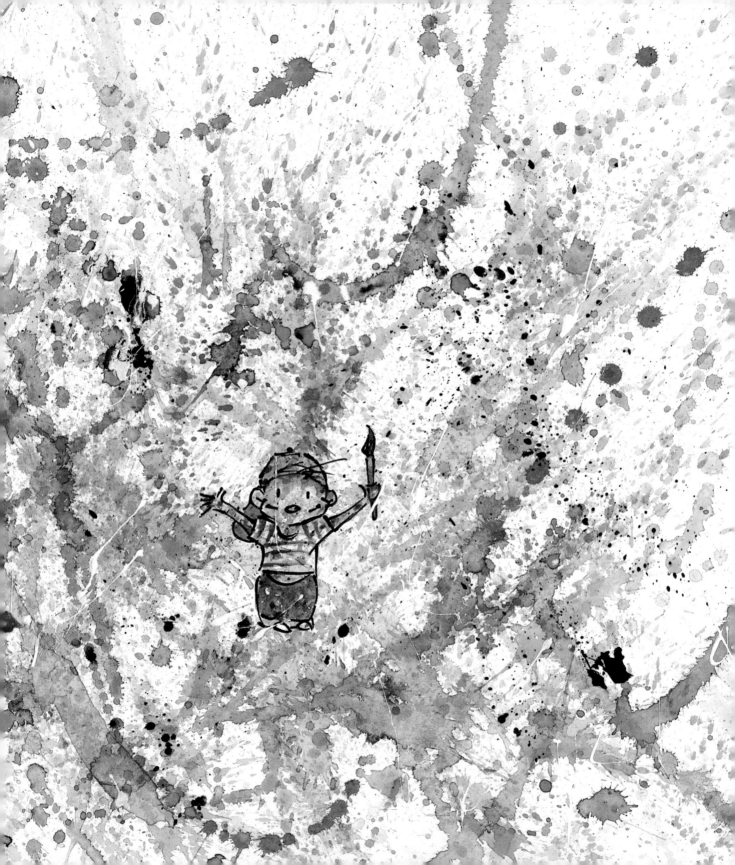

# WHEN ART IS IN PLAY

GET OUT OF ART'S WAY

HE ZIGS

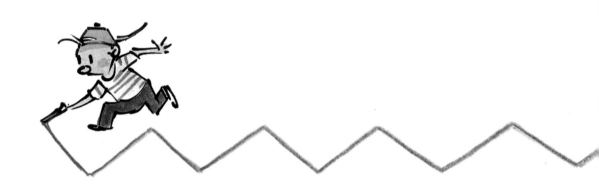

HE ZAGS

HE REALLY GETS WIRED

THERE'S NO STOPPING ART . . .

WHEN ART IS INSPIRED

# HE DRAWS SCRIBBLES

# THAT SQUIGGLE

DOTS . . .

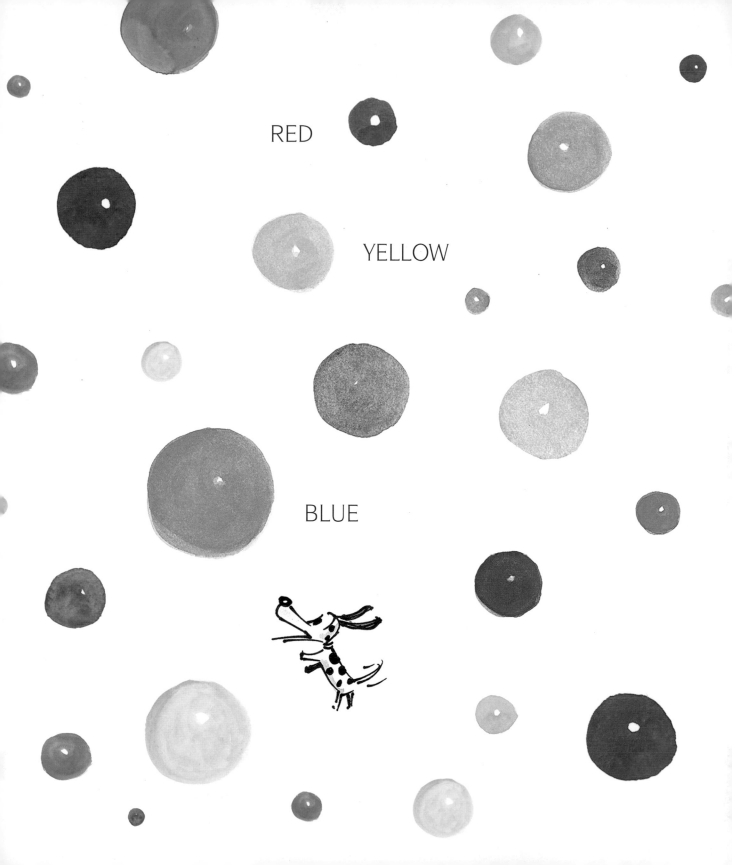

RED

YELLOW

BLUE

# SPLOTCHES

WITH BLOTCHES

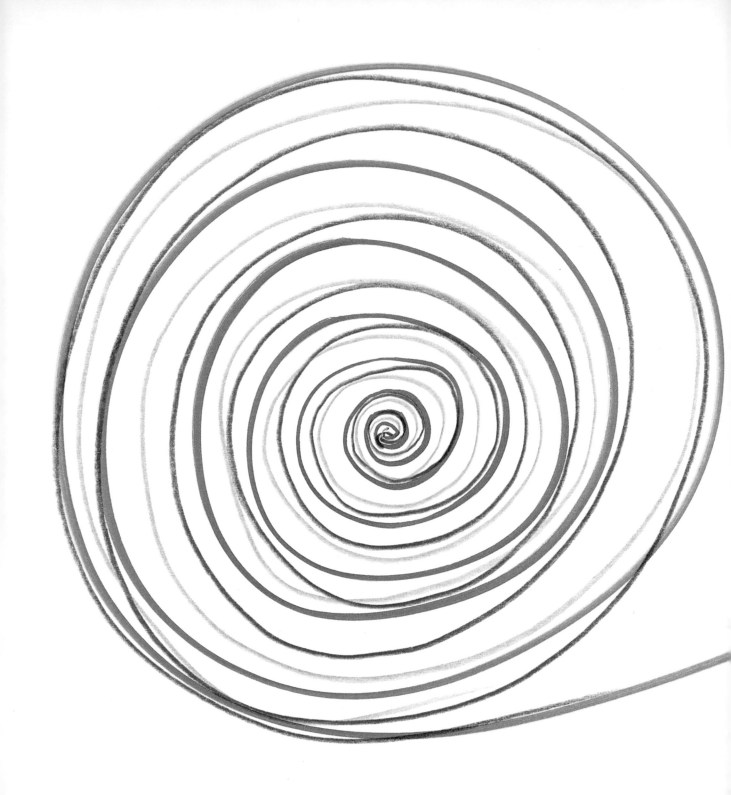

AND THE CURLIEST CUE

ART STARES AT THE PAPER

AND USES HIS NOODLE

TO CONJURE UP

A PERFECT DOODLE

# AND DOODLES NEED HOUSES

# TREES

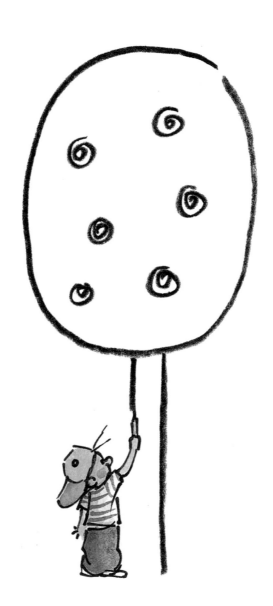

AND COOL CARS

# A DOG

# A MOON

AND A BILLION BRIGHT STARS

ART DRAWS AND DRAWS

TILL HE FLOPS IN A HEAP

AND AMONG HIS CREATIONS

HE FALLS FAST ASLEEP.

NOW LET'S BE QUIET
TO TRY SOMETHING
WE'VE HEARD . . .

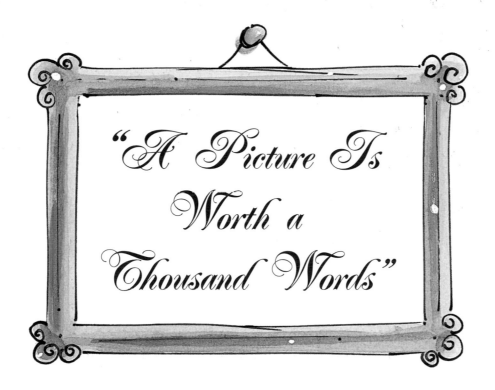

AND WHEN HE AWAKES

(A LITTLE BIT LATER)

ART SEES HIS ART

ON THE REFRIGERATOR

HELD THERE BY MAGNETS

(STARS AND A HEART)

PUT THERE BY MOTHER

'CAUSE MOTHER LOVES ART.